Amy's
Great Escape

ISBN 978-1-64349-604-7 (paperback)
ISBN 978-1-64458-252-7 (hardcover)
ISBN 978-1-64349-605-4 (digital)

Christian Faith Publishing, Inc.
832 Park Avenue
Meadville, PA 16335
www.christianfaithpublishing.com

Printed in the United States of America

Amy's Great Escape

SuzyQ

1

Who Is Amy?

Amy Brown is funny and kindhearted according to her best friend, Holly. She loves school, in the fourth grade, and says her teacher, Mr. Baker, is pretty cool too.

She has long blonde hair and blue eyes. She mostly likes to wear a ponytail, but sometimes curls it and leaves it down. She sometimes likes to get dirty helping her dad in the garage. Other times, she dresses up when going shopping with her mom.

In this story, Amy learns how to handle herself in a dangerous and scary situation. She also learns how she may have avoided it from the beginning. She finds out just how smart and strong she can be. Everyone in the town learns from Amy's experience. They learn how to be brave, to be calm, and, above all, to be strong. Not only does she show strength on the outside, but she showed strength on the inside.

Let's see if you can answer some questions during the story. You will see how well Amy uses her actions and bravery to find her way home.

3

Chapter One

It is two days before Easter and spring is finally here for this small town called Pebble Creek. Amy is excited about the holiday because on Easter Sunday the town church holds a big picnic in an open field near her house.

Amy and her parents are busy doing things around the house getting ready for Easter. Amy goes upstairs to her bedroom to find a pretty dress to wear to the picnic. Her room is pink and yellow with rainbow tie-dye pillows and curtains. She stands on the rainbow-colored fuzzy rug in front of her closet and says, "Hmmm, let's see. Maybe the yellow one will look cool and springy."

She took the outfit over to the mirror and held it in front of her then smiled and said, "Yes, this one is just right. I'm glad it is finally spring time so I can wear it."

Just then, she heard her mother call for her to come downstairs. Amy answered, "Okay. I'm coming, Mom," while skipping down the stairs.

Amy asks, "Yes, Mom?"

Mom replies, "We are having a special dinner tonight. Will you clean your room?"

Amy answered, "Sure, Mom. I'll go do it right now. Wow, that sounds great and I can't wait."

She called to her dog, "Come on, Teddy. You can keep me company." He followed behind her wagging his fluffy brown tail. Amy told Teddy,

"Maybe if I do a good job, Mom will let me color Easter eggs tonight after dinner instead of waiting until tomorrow." He just tilts his head trying to understand what she is saying.

She explains her cleaning plan to Teddy. "I'll make my bed, then straighten my books, and, last, organize my toys." Teddy followed her around the room for a little while until he landed on the fuzzy rug and decided to take a little nap.

She cleaned and cleaned until finally her room was finished. So she thought it was. Then, she asked Teddy as she looked around, "What do you think?" She was smiling at him knowing he can't answer her. Just then, Teddy walks over to a shoe that Amy didn't see lying in the corner. He picks it up with his teeth, takes it over, and drops it in front of the closet. Amy claps her hands and says, "Awesome, Teddy. What a smart boy you are." She then praised him with a pat on his head.

Amy and Teddy hurried to tell Mom that her bedroom is now super clean. Amy calls out, "Where are you, Mom?" as she coaches Teddy to follow her with a wave of her hand.

Mom answered, "I'm in the kitchen making dinner."

As Amy enters the kitchen, she says, "Do you need me to help with anything?"

Mom said, "No, honey. I have it all under control." She gave Amy a kiss and thanked her for asking.

Amy said, "Can I go out and ride my bike for a while before dinner? Oh, and can we color eggs tonight after dinner. Please?"

Mom answered, "I will check your bedroom to see how well you did in cleaning it and decide then. How's that sound?"

Amy said, "Great!" She thanked Mom with a big hug and off her and Teddy went to play.

Amy gets on her bicycle and rides down the sidewalk along Lily Drive with Teddy following behind. She saw her best friend, Holly, riding her bike too. Just then, as she brings her bike to a stop beside Amy, Holly says, "Hi, Amy. Whatcha doing?"

Amy replies, "Oh, nothing really. Just getting things ready for the big picnic on Sunday. What about you?"

Holly answered, "I just can't wait for the picnic and the big egg hunt. I heard there will be lots of prizes, a horse show, and games, and…well, I can't wait!"

Amy said, "Yeah, it's gonna be great! Hey do you want to park our bikes and sit in the grass?" Holly said, "Sure. Let's see if we could find a four-leaf clover for luck tomorrow."

While twirling her hair around her finger, Amy said, "Cool. I've never found one. Have you?"

Holly said, "Nope. Let's see who finds one first."

They both sat down on the soft green grass and began to look for at least just one lucky four-leaf clover.

Amy asked, "Hey, do you believe in the luck of a clover?"

She answered, "Well, yeah. Maybe."

Amy replies, "I believe because they are so rare and people go their whole life never finding just one."

Holly said, "I never thought about it like that before. Well then, yes I believe."

Meanwhile, Teddy found himself a nice shady spot under a tree snapping at a honey bee with his feet up in the air. The girls look over at Teddy and giggled. Amy said, "He's so silly sometimes." As she nods her head slightly, looking back down at the hundreds and hundreds of three-leaf clovers.

Suddenly, a bright red car races down the street. Both girls and Teddy look up to see this car zoom by. And just that quick, it was gone.

Holly said, "Wow, they must be in a hurry." They then went back to the clover hunt. They must have sat there for almost an hour and there was still no sign of that lucky clover anywhere. From about three houses down, Holly heard her mother calling for her to come home for dinner. She told Amy, "Well, better luck next time on finding a clover. I've got to go, but I'll see you at the picnic on Sunday." Holly got up off the grass and is about to get on her bike when she sees something right beside the front wheel. Can you guess? Yes, it's the four-leaf clover they've been looking for.

She reaches down and picks it when Amy says, "What? What is it? Did you find one? Is it the clover?"

As Holly rides away, she says, "I have to go, but I'll show it to you tomorrow. Yes, it's the clover!" Amy smiled and waved as she headed to her bike and looked around for Teddy.

Just when she saw him and was about to tell him to come home with her, he ran off chasing a cat. Amy rides her bike a few blocks away from her home to try and keep up with him. She yells, "Teddy, stop! You are going too far away." But he just wouldn't listen to Amy. She stops and parks her bike then calls for him once more, "Teddy, come here! Here, boy."

Suddenly, that same red car turns the corner and is headed down the street. But this time, it is moving slowly. As the car gets closer and closer to Amy, the window comes down and a voice from the car says, "Do you want help getting your dog? I am real good with animals."

Amy answered, "No. Thank you, sir. I am not supposed to talk to strangers." Then she started to walk away.

The man said, "Well, my name is Jack and I work for the animal shelter. See, we're not strangers now." As the man stops the car and gets out, Amy thought to herself *He seems nice, so maybe he can help me get Teddy.*

He had brown hair, a mustache, and didn't look mean. The man tells Amy, "Look, your dog has trapped a cat in that tree. Come on, we will get him. What's your dog's name anyway?"

Amy is distracted by the conversation and forgets about being cautious of this stranger and says, "His name is Teddy."

They both call to Teddy as he is busy barking at the cat. Soon, he stopped and came to Amy. She scooped him up and fussed at him for not coming when she called him. As she walks back to her bike, the man follows and says, "I'm really glad you got your dog back. Do you want a ride home? I can put your bike in my trunk."

Amy said, "Oh, no. Thank you for your help though."

She put Teddy down and was about to get on her bike when all of a sudden the man grabs her. He covers her mouth and pushes her in the car. After shaking Teddy off of his pant leg and then locking the car doors, he starts the car and takes off as fast as lightning. Amy is terrified and screamed as loud as she can but nobody can hear except Teddy. He runs after the car as far as his little legs would take him, barking for all to hear. But the car is fading out of Teddy's sight now and he must go back home.

Teddy knew something was terribly wrong, so he runs as fast as he could to try and tell Mom and Dad. Teddy scratches on the door in a panic to alert someone. Finally, Mom opens the door, looks down, and says, "Well, hello, Teddy. Where is Amy and why are you shaking?" He is frantically barking and pacing back and forth. As Mom looks up and out across the lawn, Mom asks Teddy, "Is something wrong? Where is Amy?"

Mrs. Brown calls for her husband to come. Mr. Brown came to the front door and said, "Yes, dear. What do you need?"

She replied, "I don't see Amy anywhere and Teddy was by himself."

Mr. Brown stepped out to the porch and took a good look around then called out, "Amy! Amy! Where are you?"

Poor Teddy. He knew what happened but was unable to tell them. All he could do is whimper because he just lost his very best friend.

Mrs. Brown told her husband, "Maybe she just went to Holly's house or one of her other friends."

Mr. Brown said, "Well, let's walk down there and see. There is no reason to worry until there is something to worry about."

Mrs. Brown said, "You are right, honey."

Teddy followed as they began walking down the sidewalk yelling for their daughter as they went. Soon, Mr. Brown saw Amy's bike lying on the ground near a tree. As they approached the bike, Teddy started barking louder and louder. Now, they are beginning to worry because not only did they find Amy's bike on the ground but her bracelet was also on the ground. Mr. Brown picked up the bicycle and the bracelet and they immediately went to Holly's home to find out if anyone has seen Amy recently.

Holly answers the door and says, "Oh, hi, Mr. and Mrs. Brown." While looking around, she says, "Where is Amy?"

Mr. and Mrs. Brown stood still. They looked at one another in hesitation. Mr. Brown says, "Holly, we really were hoping you would be able to tell us where Amy is. Have you seen her today and if so, where?"

Holly answered in a hurry, "Yes, I saw her not long ago. We parked our bikes and sat on the grass while we talked and searched for a four-leaf clover."

Mr. and Mrs. Jackson (Holly's parents) walked up behind Holly to see who is at the door. Mr. Jackson says, "Oh, hello, Mr. and Mrs. Brown."

Mrs. Jackson says, "Come on in. Would you like a cup of coffee?"

Mr. and Mrs. Brown just looked at each other and said at the same time, "We are looking for Amy."

Mr. Brown said, "We found her bike and her bracelet on the ground and Teddy came home alone upset."

Mrs. Brown said, "We don't know what to do and we're beginning to worry."

Mr. Jackson said, "Okay, Mr. Brown and I will go door to door to see if anyone has seen her. You and Mrs. Brown stay here and call her friends and tell them we will gather at the church in one hour."

Mr. Brown told them he will call the pastor and ask him to hold a town meeting. He then hugged his wife and told her it will be alright and that they we will find her.

She kissed him on the cheek and said, "I know. I have faith."

Mrs. Jackson asked Mrs. Brown to have a seat on the sofa as she gets them something to drink. Mrs. Brown said, "Thank you. I am going to make calls to her classmates beginning with her teacher, Miss Bird." Holly is also busy calling everyone she can think of while petting Teddy and telling him it will be okay.

Mr. Brown and Mr. Jackson returned to the house to explain to the women that nobody in the neighborhood has seen her. Amy's mom and dad hugged each other tight and whispered together, "Let's pray."

Chapter Two

It has been over an hour since Amy was home with her family. During the ride, she has taken peeks out the window to look for something familiar. So far, she remembers seeing a sign to a restaurant she's been to across town. After he got onto the freeway, she remembered a number forty-five on a sign.

The scary, dark-haired, and scruffy-faced man has not said a word. Repeatedly, Amy has begged the man to take her home. He says nothing at all. With tears pouring down her face, she asks desperately once again, "Please, mister. Oh, please take me home."

The man finally replies, "We are pulling up to your new home now. You will like it here."

She inches up to the window in fear but curiosity and slowly peeks out.

When the car came to a stop, the man quickly turns around and says, "Now, listen up, girl. I'm not here to hurt you as long as you do what you are told. First, what is your name?"

Amy tries to speak but the words just won't come out. She is crying so hard she can't get her breath to talk.

The man's voice got loud, "You'd better tell me your name now!"

Amy stutters it the best she can, "A-A-A-Amy."

The man said, "Well, that's more like it. See, we will get along just fine. Now, the second thing is that when we go into the house, you will meet my wife, Nancy. She has wanted a little girl for a long, long time. So, it's important that you are nice to her. Do you understand?"

Amy slowly looks up and says, "Yes, I will be nice." She then puts her head back down because she just can't look at his mean face. What she would like to say would probably make him mad. So she stays as calm as she can.

The man said, "And the third thing is don't try and escape because you will be sorry. Also, if you take a look around, there is no place to go."

Poor Amy. She was so scared and so sad as she slowly looks out the back window to see nothing but trees.

The man tells her that he knows where her parents are and if she wants to keep them safe, she needs to do what he says. Now, Amy is thinking she may never see her mom and dad again.

Do you think there is a way for Amy to escape and keep her and her parents safe too? Keep reading and you will find out just how she does it.

The man, named Jack, is about to escort Amy into the strange house to meet a strange woman named Nancy. He tells her, "Now, come on. Let's go in and meet your new mom. She has been waiting for this day for a very long time. Just remember what I said. Be nice or else."

Amy slowly moves to the edge of the seat at the opened car door and puts her feet on the ground. She slowly looks up and around and saw the house. Jack looks down at her and says, "How do you like it?"

Of course Amy does not answer him as she is still crying and scared.

He takes her hand and holds it tight while pulling her along. Amy thinks to herself, *Stay calm. Look at the house for a way out...like the windows, the roof, and the door.* She walks very slowly while pulling back on his hold. She looks for more details, like the driveway to the main road or if there are any signs popping up behind the trees and what direction they are.

In the middle of her scoping out the area, without him knowing, a large dog comes running and barking at her. He is huge compared to her sweet little Teddy, which reminds her how much she misses him. Jack calls the dog "Hooch" and says, "Hooch, stay down! He won't bother you as long as I'm around."

She puts her hand out slowly and lets him smell it without bending into his face. The dog licks her hand as they are still walking almost to the door when it suddenly opens. There stands a woman with old torn clothes and light brown hair who said, "Oh, my. Isn't she perfect?" As she glanced at her and gave him a hug, she said, "Thank you, my love. Now I have a daughter of my own."

Then, she bent down at Amy and said, "You don't have to be sad. We are going to take good care of you. Now, let me see a smile."

Amy just stood there welling up in tears and said, "Ma'am, I just want to go home. Please, please can I go home?"

The woman takes her other hand and says, "But, darling. You are home now in your new home. Come on. I'll show you your new bedroom."

Amy knew these strangers are not taking her home and that it was up to her if she is to escape. Jack let's go of Amy's hand and Nancy tugs on the other one.

All Amy can think of is staying calm as hard as it is then pay close attention to details as she enters the house. Barely inside the door, she looks up and is standing in the living room. Over to the left is the kitchen, where she sees a side door. She immediately looks around to see if there is a phone of any kind, which might be lying on a table. She also looks for any weapons and any keys that they might have. The house is very messy and doesn't smell very good. Amy continues to keep her eyes on everything as Nancy takes her to the bedroom upstairs. She pays close attention while walking up the stairs to noises that each step makes. As she follows behind, Amy notices that the third step from the top does make a creaking sound. This she must remember.

When they reached the top of the stairs, Amy sees a door on the left and on the right. Nancy walks toward the door on the left, which is further down the hall. She notices what looks like a closet door or maybe a bathroom. However, Nancy doesn't open that door. She opens the bedroom door as Amy slowly approaches and says, "This is your room, honey. Oh, I forgot to ask you your name. Well, it doesn't matter because your new name is, I hope you like it, Melinda."

Amy says, "But my name is Amy, not Melinda."

Nancy replies, "Yes, but I want people to know you as Melinda. You will have our last name and be our little girl from now on."

Amy just looks around the room and thinks to herself, *Stay calm it's no use to fight with them.* So, she looks around the room and sees the bed directly facing the door with an old quilt cover on it. The dresser is over on the right wall and is all scuffed up with scratches. Above the dresser is a nailed board covering up the window.

Nancy says with excitement as she opens one of the dresser drawers, "Look, I even have you some nice clothes to wear."

Just when Amy looked in to see the clothes, she sees a bug running over them. She shivered a bit and told the woman as she slowly looked behind her at Jack "Yes, those are nice."

At this point, Amy knows she is going to have to playact and try and think more like a grown up.

I have faith in her. Don't you? Amy has taken in a whole lot of information that she must try and remember. Soon, you will find out what Amy does to remember every detail she has learned. It's gotten late and dark outside. She must stay positive and believe that she can overcome this horrible nightmare.

Nancy sits on the bed and says, "Come. Sit down so we can talk, Melinda."

Amy moves slowly and sits down beside the woman as Jack goes downstairs. Nancy says, "Tell me all about yourself, hon."

Amy wasn't sure how to start a conversation with her so she said, "Well, I like to ride my bike and hang out with my best friend, Holly. I like to draw too. Can I have some paper and a pencil?"

Nancy said, "Sure, you can draw. Maybe it will help you settle in here. I'll go get you some right now as long as you stay here in this room."

Amy replied, "Yes ma'am, I will."

When the woman left the room, Amy started crying again. She just couldn't help it. She is just so sad. She dried up her tears and wiped her face when she heard the woman coming back.

When she came in the room, she said, "Here you are. It's a lot of paper and I found you some colored pencils. Will this do, Melinda?"

Amy answered, "Yes, thank you for being so nice to me. I am really tired. If it's okay, I'd like to lay down for a while."

Nancy said as she stroked Amy's hair, "Of course, Melinda. You must be very tired. I will go and prepare supper for all of us and call you when it's ready, okay?"

Amy replied, "Okay."

Nancy kept the door open as she walked away. After Amy heard the woman go downstairs, she quickly wrote down everything that she remembered about her surroundings. She also wrote down a detailed description of Nancy and Jack and their home. Now that she has all that information written down, she must put it in a place where they will not find it because if they do, there is no telling what could happen to her then. So, she folded it up and placed it in the only safe place she could think of. Yep, in her underwear. Then, she drew a picture of a flower and laid it on the bedside table so the woman would see that she did draw something. She laid her head down on the lumpy pillow and closed her eyes not to go to sleep even though she is super tired but to visualize her family. She misses them so bad that it brings her to tears once again. She gets up, kneels beside the bed, and begins to pray.

"Lord, help me get back to my family. I need them and they need me. That's how it's supposed to be. With all of your love and all your might, I need you to help me escape tonight. Amen."

23

After her prayer, she climbed back on the bed and thought *I am going to need strength both mentally and physically. So even though I don't want to or think I can, I need to try and take a nap and eat some food later. If I don't, I might miss my chance by getting weak or falling asleep in the night.* Amy closed her eyes and whispered quietly, "Momma and Daddy, I will make it home God is going to help me. You'll see. I love you. I love you. I love you." Amy drifted off to sleep while softly saying those words over and over.

Downstairs in the kitchen while Nancy is finishing up supper, she and Jack are discussing their next move. This is to leave town with their new daughter. They have been planning to find a little girl to kidnap for a long time. It was unfortunate for Amy to be so trusting, but fortunate for them she was. They decide that Sunday would be the time to leave. This would give them time to pack their things. Tomorrow, they will spend the day with "Melinda" to get her prepared for her new forever home.

Nancy asks Jack, "Do you think we can make her like us?"

Jack answered, "Sure. It will take a little time but before you know it, she will forget all about her other life. If she gives us trouble though, I will put her in her place."

Nancy replied, "She will be good, I'm sure of it. I'm going to call her for dinner now."

Jack opens up his second beer and sits down to the kitchen table while Nancy goes up to get "Melinda." She finds her sleeping while hugging the pillow. On her face is an undried tear resting on her cheek. Nancy smiles and softly says, "You will learn to love us. Just wait and see, Melinda."

Amy jumped frantically when she heard the name that doesn't belong to her. She quickly sat up, folded her legs to her chest, and said, "Please don't hurt me!"

Nancy said, "I just came to get you for dinner. I'm not going to hurt the newest member of our family. Now, I promised Jack you would be good. Let's not make him mad."

Amy couldn't stand the smell of her breath as she spoke. She thinks it might be alcohol.

Nancy noticed the drawing of a flower on the table and said, "How pretty this is. Can I have it, Melinda?"

Amy said, "Yes. I made it for you because you've been kind and nice."

Nancy said, "Oh, thank you. Now let's go eat dinner before it gets cold."

Amy is walking toward the stairs following Nancy and reminds herself that she needs to pay attention to any squeaky steps going down because she knows which one squeaks going up. She walks on the opposite side of Nancy so she can hear squeaks coming from her steps too. Since no steps made a noise in Nancy's path, then that's the path she's taking. When they reached the living room, Amy says, "Ma'am, may I use the restroom, please?"

Nancy answered with a chuckle, "Of course, you can. I'm sorry I didn't show you that room. Oh, and you can call me Nancy for now. Maybe someday you will like me enough to call me mom."

Amy thought to herself, *In your dreams maybe.*

She goes into the bathroom to splash water on her face to help clear her mind. Amy knows she has a very long night ahead of her and the cold water will refresh her senses. She washes her hands, looks straight into the mirror, and says, "You can do this. By staying calm, you can make your way back home."

She walks out of the bathroom and before going into the kitchen, where Nancy and Jack are, she takes another look around the living room. Just then, she sees an addressed envelope with both of their names on it. She slowly and quietly grabs it up and steps back into the bathroom. She eases the door closed and folds up the envelope then puts it in her underwear along with her notes. Just then, she hears Nancy call out, "Is everything okay, Melinda?"

After jumping a little, Amy answered quickly, "Yes, I'm coming."

As she hurries to the kitchen, she finds them both drinking beer and laughing at the table.

Jack turned and saw Amy then said, "Well, hello, sleepy head. Come and join us. Nancy, get the girl a beer."

He just laughs at the look on Amy's face and said, "Ha, I'm just kidding you, kid. Ha, ha! Get it kid-ding? Come on in and sit down at the table. We are having pinto beans and cornbread. Yum-yum."

Amy, with her crooked smile, just tilted her head and did what she was told. Nancy just shook her head and said, "You can't pay attention to that old fool. He's about half drunk. Give me another hour and I will be too. He, he."

Amy didn't say a word as Nancy plopped a spoon of beans in the bowl in front of her. Although Amy is not fond of pinto beans, she does in fact like cornbread. She knows she will have to nourish her body in order to keep up her strength for the journey ahead so she finished it all.

During the meal, there was very little conversation. Every now and then, Jack and Nancy would both look up at each other, smile, and snicker. This just made Amy mad on the inside. In fact, she went from being sad and scared to mad and brave after watching these adults act like children. Suddenly, Jack slammed his hand on the table, looked at Amy, and said, "Speak up, girl! Don't you have anything to say?"

Amy did jump a little then said, "I'm sorry. I'm just really tired and sleepy. Can I go back to the bedroom and take a piece of cornbread too? It was real good."

After taking another big drink of his beer, he answered, "Get the cornbread and go!" as he pointed his finger toward the steps. Amy got up slowly and walked away.

Nancy asks, "Do you want me to come with you, dear? There are pajamas in the dresser drawer for you." Her voice got louder as Amy walked slowly into the living room.

She answered, "No. Thank you, ma'am, I mean Nancy. Thank you for dinner. It was good."

Nancy yells with a slur in her voice, "Okay. We will see you bright and early in the morning with a surprise for you!"

Amy thinks to herself, *Yeah, you are the one who is going to have a surprise in the morning because I won't be here.*

She is approaching the steps when she spotted a weapon on the bookcase to the right. She goes up to the bedroom and closes the door but leaves it open just enough to hear them coming up the stairs.

It is important that Amy never drops her guard and stays on alert at all times. Amy has stayed in control of the situation by making them think she has accepted the situation. Because of Amy's great acting, they are the ones who are dropping their guards and not on alert.

During the story, you should picture yourself being in this situation or simply ask your parents if they will practice a kidnapping play with you. Now, Amy never had any self-defense classes, which would have been helpful at the beginning. But it is most helpful to learn calming techniques in case self-defense doesn't work and the criminal overpowers you.

Amy takes out her notes and adds other important facts. She knows it will be hard but she has to stay awake no matter what. She sits on the bed and writes every detail of every move she will make. If you are like Amy, writing stuff down helps you remember. Now, all the while she is writing, she is on alert and ready to quietly fold the paper and stash it.

She can still hear them laughing and giggling downstairs. She believes it will be quite a while before they finally pass out from the alcohol. She is just hoping that happens in their bed upstairs. It will be a lot harder to sneak past them if they are on the couch. Either way, she has decided that trying is better than not trying. Also, she has a plan of what to do and say if she where to get caught. You will find out what that is later.

Chapter Three

Meanwhile, back at Amy's hometown of Pebble Creek, everyone from the neighborhood has gathered at the church for prayer and to support her friends and family. It has been a very difficult two hours because there is no sign of Amy anywhere. Family and friends went all over town to look for her. They went door to door. They went to the park and even to the businesses in town. People drove around calling her name out the window. They stopped others on the street asking about her but nobody has seen Amy.

Amy's parents, Mr. and Mrs. Brown (Jim and Sally), sat quietly with tears in their eyes unknowing where to look next. Mr. Brown stands up and helps his wife up and says, "Honey, it is time we go to the police."

Mrs. Brown wiped her tears and said, "You are right. Let's go."

When Pastor Adams saw Jim and Sally standing, he walked over to them and asked, "What more can we do? I speak for everyone who is still here for you and your little girl."

Sally replied, "There isn't much any of us can do now that it's so dark. I think they all should go home and get rest for now."

Jim agreed adding, "Would you mind making an announcement encouraging them to go home? Let them know how grateful we are and if they'd like to help continue the search at first light to meet back here."

The pastor said, "I absolutely will. I know it will be hard, but you both should also try and rest some before morning."

Jim thanked Pastor Adams and they were off to the police station.

During the car ride, aside from the sad sound of sniffles, there was silence. When they were almost there, Sally spoke in a quivering voice while looking out the window and said, "I'm so worried that our little Amy is out there in the cold, lost and hungry."

Jim said, "Hey, look at me. She is strong and very independent. Remember the first time we took her fishing and how she was determined to bait her own hook on the fishing pole? Well, she did perfect and did not hurt herself. And then, if you remember she got a decent-sized fish on that hook and wouldn't even let me help her reel it in."

Sally made a half smile and put her hand on his face and said, "I remember. I also remember that you and I didn't catch a thing. She couldn't wait to set that fish free and watch it swim off."

Jim stroked her hair and gave her a big hug and said, "Come on. Let's go in and file a report. We've prayed that the Lord will bring her home safe and it's our job to have faith."

Sally gently nodded her head in agreement as she opened the car door.

They went in and asked to speak to a detective right away. The officer at the front desk said, "What seems to be the problem?"

Jim explained, and the officer immediately took them to meet Detective Smith. The officer said, "Detective Smith, this is Mr. and Mrs. Brown. They say their daughter is missing and need to file a report."

Detective Smith stood up, shook each of their hands, and asked them to have a seat. He said, "First, I want to tell you that my department and I will do everything possible to find your daughter. Now, let's start by you telling me the story."

Jim and Sally explained everything they knew to Detective Smith. He asked them, "Do you have a recent picture of your daughter?"

Sally answered as she hands him her phone, "I do have a photo but it's here on my phone. Can you print it from here or do we need to get one from home?"

He said, "She is a very pretty young girl. Yes, I can send it to our printer from here."

The detective took her phone and Jim took her hand. He looked at her and whispered, "It will be alright. You'll see, sweetheart."

She gave him a smile and squeezed his hand.

After just a few minutes, the detective came back to his desk and told them he has everything they need. He also suggested that they should go home and get some rest. He said, "I have put out an APB Amber alert and we will call you with any updates. Please try not to worry. We will find her."

Jim and Sally headed home, but even though it wasn't a long drive, to them it sure felt like one. When they pulled into the driveway, the first thing they see is Amy's bicycle propped against the house. Somehow, they have to go into that empty house and take their empty hearts with them. Sally takes a deep breath and says, "Come on. I'll make us some coffee because I know we are not going to be able to sleep."

Sally puts on the coffee and Jim puts on the news. When Sally opens the refrigerator, she sees the boiled eggs that she and Amy were going to color. She tears up for just a minute and reminds herself to have faith. She fixes their coffee and takes it into the living room. They sat on the sofa and leaned on each other for a while and then a knock came at the door.

Jim said, "I'll get it. You relax."

Sally quickly replied, "No way. I'm coming with you."

When he opened the door, there stood Mr. and Mrs. Jackson (Sam and Debbie).

Sam said, "We couldn't sleep either."

Jim invited them in and Sally brought them a cup of coffee.

Debbie said, "We decided to come over when we saw that your lights were still on. We couldn't relax until we knew how you were. We also wanted to tell you that Holly is taking good care of Teddy. They fell asleep together not long ago. It was so cute."

Sally gave a short smile and said, "How sweet. Tell Holly we thank her for all her help. We thank you both for coming over and for helping the search tonight. I just keep watching the clock and looking out the window, wishing for daylight."

Sam asked, "Jim, is there anything you need me to do?"

Jim thought for a few seconds and replied, "You know, as a matter of fact, there is something you can help me do. I want to create a small poster with Amy's picture on it and make several copies so we can post them around town."

Sam said, "That is a great idea. I would like to help in any way I can."

Sally agreed by saying, "That is a wonderful idea."

She looked at Debbie and said, "I just thought of something you and I could do if you want."

Debbie replied, "Of course, anything at all."

Sally explained, "Well, because of our strong faith that Amy will be coming home, I would like to do something for Amy. See, we were going to color Easter eggs together for the big hunt on Sunday…"

Jim interrupted and said, "That's right. She was so excited about that."

Sally continued, "I thought we could color them for her as a surprise."

Debbie took her hand and said, "I think that is a nice thing to do and I would love to help."

Sally and Debbie went into the kitchen and Jim and Sam went into the office.

So Jim and Sally found something positive to do in a negative situation with the help of true friends. See, nothing happens unless you make it happen. They all decided that doing something is better than doing nothing. Morning will surely come sooner now that they aren't watching the clock.

Having faith brings so much peace and comfort into a bad situation. It could be faith in a Christian way, faith in a friend, or even faith in yourself. Do you think that Amy has gained enough faith and confidence in herself to do what she is about to do? Let's find out.

Chapter Four

Back at the old scary house, Amy has been waiting patiently for Jack and Nancy to fall sound asleep. It has been very hard for her to stay awake, especially when she has to pretend to be asleep every time Nancy peeks in on her. But Amy knows that her plan will not work if she isn't patient. In order to help her stay awake, she only closes her eyes when she hears Nancy coming. She does silly things to keep her mind active, like use her finger to trace the pattern on the quilt. Sometimes, she points her finger to the ceiling and draws an imaginary picture. It has been quite a while since Nancy checked on her.

Amy's plan to escape is about to happen. She runs it through her mind over and over. She knows she cannot make any mistakes. Her heart is racing like a race horse in the lead. She doesn't take out her notes until she is positive, without a doubt, that they are both sound asleep. It has been nearly two hours since she heard them talking in the bedroom down the hall. She must have a backup plan just in case one of them wakes up and catches her. She is thankful that they fell asleep in the bedroom instead of on the sofa in the living room. The hardest part will be to sneak past their bedroom without making a sound.

It is time! She takes out her notes and goes over everything once again in her mind. She puts the notes back in her underwear, takes a deep breath, grabs the square of cornbread, and tiptoes to the door. (Do you know why she got the cornbread? Keep reading and you will see.)

Now, the door was never closed so she doesn't have to worry about it squeaking. She just slides carefully around it. She stands very still for a few seconds to listen closely. She hears a faint sound of slow breathing and nothing else from their bedroom. She knows just what to say if they awaken and catch her walking down the steps.

Do you know what she can say? If your answer is going to the bathroom, you are right. Of course, she can only use that excuse until she gets past the bathroom. She will not be going out the front door because it is too close to their bedroom. Therefore, she will be going by leaving out of the side door in the kitchen. So if they were to catch her in the kitchen, what excuse could she say? If your answer is getting something to drink with my cornbread, you are right. She will have the cornbread in her hand to show them. That makes it more believable. The cornbread has another purpose. Soon, you'll see.

So far, Amy has avoided the squeaky steps and made it to the bottom. She remembered the weapon on the bookcase and took a T-shirt from the arm of a chair and gently laid it on the weapon. (Do you know why?) Because it would make it harder to find and confuse Jack on where he placed it. (Now, not all situations would allow for this technique to work but it does in Amy's situation.) She then stops and listens. She can still hear them breathing but just barely. (Why doesn't Amy just start walking fast toward the door and get out of there?) If you said because that is not staying calm, you would be right. She has made it past the bathroom and is now standing in the kitchen and can see the door to her great escape. Once again, she stands very quiet and listens for noises coming from behind. She knows that when she is standing at that door with her hand on the knob, there is no excuse to give them.

This is it—the moment that really counts. She has to do this last part super-duper carefully. She quietly opens the door and steps out, turns around, and quietly closes the door. Suddenly, she hears something. The door is closed and something is outside. Yep, it's that dog! She remembered and put down on her notes that she would have to deal with that dog. So, guess what? She whispered his name, which she also put in her notes, "Hooch, look I have cornbread." She broke it in half and quickly gave him a piece. She started walking quietly away from the house, toward the driveway, and here comes Hooch wanting more. She showed him the other half and threw it as far as she could behind the house. Then, she took off running down the driveway as fast as she could. Amy never stopped running until she got to the main road and that horrible house was out of sight.

She stops to catch her breath and with such relief she said, "Finally, I'm in the clear. I can't believe I actually did it!"

She looks up into the moonlit sky and says, "Thank you, God. You made sure they didn't wake, you made sure I didn't trip over something and wake them up, you made sure that Hooch didn't bark or attack me, and you made sure I had this beautiful moonlight to light my way to that gas station sign I see popping up behind the trees. You are the greatest!"

She walked and walked down that lonely road in the dark but she never got scared. She never once felt like she was alone. Do you know why? If you said one of these things: because she felt calm or that God was with her or that she was way more scared before. You are right.

Amy's faith continued to rise with every step she took down that road. She just started singing a happy song, "Frosty the snowman was a jolly happy soul. With corn cob pipe and a button nose and two eyes made out of coal."

Even though she was tired, cold, and her feet hurt like crazy, she was confident that she would be back with her family soon so she didn't even think about those things. (Can Amy relax and drop her guard or should she still be alert to the possibility of danger?) If you said no, she should stay alert, you are right.

She is not far from the gas station now and can see it all lit up. She whispers to herself with excitement, "I'm almost there!"

Just then, she hears a car from a distance and turns around. Yep, sure enough, those are headlights about to shine on her. She thinks fast. Just before the car comes around the curve, the headlight misses her as she ducks behind a bush on the side of the road. She waits until the car passes and slowly comes out from the bush. (The reason Amy didn't want the car to see her is what if it were those kidnappers?) She isn't taking any chances. She continues on to the gas station, but now she is running. That experience made her just a bit scared.

She is coming into the parking lot where she can see a few people putting gas in their cars. She runs right past all of them and into the store. Completely out of breath, she runs up to the counter and shouts, "Sir, Sir!" She swallows and takes a deep breath then continues, "I was kidnapped yesterday from my neighborhood. Please call the police so they can take me home."

The man behind the counter just looked at her and said, "Ah, ah…well, honey. Come back here with me and I'll call Officer Stewart. He just left here. He spoke of a little girl who was missing. Are you Amy?"

Amy started around the counter and said, "Yes, I am Amy Brown and I live at 1964 Lily Drive. I am so tired. Can I please just sit here on the floor and wait for the officer?"

He grabbed his phone and dialed the officers' number then bent down, patted her on the head, and said, "I'm calling him right now."

The store man finished serving a few customers then went to the back room and brought out a blanket to wrap around Amy. She finally feels safe enough to lay her head over a box and close her eyes for a minute.

It wasn't long when Officer Stewart arrived at the store to see Amy exhausted curled up in the corner behind the counter. He bent down and gently rubbed her arm and said, "Amy, Amy Brown?"

She jumped up, rubbed her eyes, and reached out both arms to what appeared to be a superman. He scooped her up and said, "Are you hurt anywhere?"

She said in a low voice as she began to cry, "No. I just want to go home."

He replied calmly, "Well, honey. That is just where we are going." Officer Stewart thanked the store clerk, gave him a wink, and told him he will see him later. He gently places her in the front seat of the car and buckles her in. She lays over the arm rest and falls back to sleep.

Chapter Five

The sun is beginning to rise at 1964 Lily Drive. The Browns and the Jacksons have been together all night eagerly waiting for that morning light to shine. The men completed making the poster flyers to place around town. The women finished decorating all of the eggs. Waiting for daylight was the only thing stopping them from continuing their search for Amy.

Sally is about to go to the window when her phone rings. Sally shouts, "Hey, everyone. It's the police station!" She is worried what the officer might say so she quickly hands the phone to her husband and says, "Here, you answer it please. I just can't."

Jim takes the phone and answers it, "Hello. Yes, this is Mr. Brown."

The voice said, "This is Officer Stewart. I have very good news for you, sir. It's about your daughter."

Jim immediately took the phone from his face and put the speaker on for all to hear and said, "We are listening, officer."

The voice continued, "Your daughter is safe with me and we'll be arriving at your home in a few minutes." The officer could hear yells and screams of joy over that call.

Sally grabbed the phone and said, "Oh, thank you, officer. We will wait for you."

They simply couldn't wait inside so they were standing on the front porch when Amy and the officer pulled up. With tears of overwhelming joy, Sally ran to hug her precious little girl.

Amy whispered in a tired voice, "Mom, I missed you all so much."

Jim reached in and picked her up and headed to the house. Sally followed her husband as he laid her down on the sofa.

The Jacksons asked the officer to come in for coffee. Amy was so tired from the terrifying experience. She could just barely keep her eyes open. Everyone is feeling blessed with a miracle.

Officer Stewart needs to get a statement from Amy but he knows she is simply too exhausted to do that right now. He told them he would be back later after Amy gets rest for the story.

Amy popped up and said, "Wait, I have what you need to catch those people. They said if I escape they will come back here and get me and my family." Amy pulls out the envelope from her hiding place and hands it to the officer.

He looks at it and says, "What a smart girl you are. This has their name and address on it. I will send a car here to watch your house and send another to arrest Mr. and Mrs. Gains."

Before closing her eyes again, Amy said, "Hey, Superman. Thank you for keeping us all safe."

The officer gave her a wink and said, "You get rest, little brave one. I'll see you later."

46

Amy hugs her parents just before she drifted back to sleep on the sofa. Dad leans over to carry her to bed when she softly said, "No. Dad can I stay here with you and Mom, please." So, Mom sat down and put Amy's head in her lap and Dad sat on the other end with her legs in his.

Mr. Jackson told Mr. Brown that he would contact Pastor Adams so he can spread the word that Amy is home safe. Then he and his wife went home to also get rest. Amy kept saying in her sleep, "I am home. I am home."

Amy and her parents fell asleep together on the sofa and slept until the afternoon.

Mom and Amy started waking up and then Dad. Mom went to the kitchen to bring Amy a glass of milk. Dad yawned and put his arm around his daughter and said, "You had us worried my little princess."

Amy replied, "Believe me, I was worried too." She started to cry and said, "I was so afraid I would never see you again."

Mom came in and said, "It is simple. The Lord answered our prayers and helped you come back to us."

The rest of the day was spent enjoying time with each other. Amy explained the entire story to her parents and Officer Stewart when he later stopped by. Holly and her parents came to visit Amy and of course she brought Teddy.

Teddy was so excited to see Amy you would have thought he was going to wag his tail off his butt. Pastor Adams told Amy that the big Easter egg hunt will be set for next Sunday. He said, "This will give you time to rest up for it."

Amy stood up and said, "Pastor Adams, I feel great. I just needed some sleep. That's all. Can we please have the picnic tomorrow?"

He answered, "Well, if your parents think you are up for it. Then let's do it."

Amy smiled at them, and they both nodded their heads yes. Everyone left to prepare for the big church picnic.

Amy tells Mom she is going to hurry and take a quick bath so she will have time to color the Easter eggs. Mom takes Amy into the kitchen and shows her all the colored eggs ready for the hunt. Amy said, "Oh, Mom. They are beautiful. How did you know I would be home and we would still go to the picnic?"

Mom said, "Faith. That's how I knew."

She kissed and hugged her daughter and told her to go take a nice long bubble bath. Mom and Dad teamed up in the kitchen and made Amy her favorite meal. Later, they watched a funny movie and ate popcorn. When it was time for bed, they snuggled together and slept all night long.

Morning came and off to church they went. Pastor Adams gave a huge thanks and praise to the Lord for bringing Amy home safe and sound. After the wonderful service, the picnic and big surprise began. Amy doesn't know it but, this picnic is now in her honor. Holly has a special surprise for her BFF too. The officer Amy called Superman will also have something for her.

Amy's dad was instructed to cover her eyes as she walks out of the church and into the back field. When she gets there, he uncovers her eyes

and she hears, "Surprise!" Then she looks up and sees a huge banner that say's "Welcome Home, Amy." This made Amy feel so special, like the whole town loved her. Officer Stewart walked up to Amy and told her that those people are in jail and would never bother her again. She thanked him and told him that now she feels a lot better.

He said, "Amy, it is you we want to thank. If it weren't for that envelope and your notes, we may have never found them." He took her hand and escorted her up onto the platform in front of all the people. There, he told all about her bravery and how children can overcome bad things. He turned to her and gave her a ribbon for bravery.

Everyone waited to greet Amy and express their love.

Holly found Amy in the crowd and told her she had a special surprise for her. First, she gave her a hug and then she handed her a present. Amy smiled at her as she opened it. There, in a beautiful frame, was the four-leaf clover that Holly found just before the terrible incident. Amy just stared at it and couldn't speak through her tears of happiness. Then she said, "I love you, Holly. You really are my best friend forever!"

Amy looked up at her parents and said, "I will be right back. There is something that I need to do."

She walked to the platform and lowered the microphone and made a speech that none of them will forget. "Kids all over the world and of all ages should be taught how to fight for their freedom. Don't ever believe what a criminal tells you. He told me that if I try to escape, he knows where I live and will hurt me and my family. Well, here I am, standing free. (The crowd applauded). There are techniques that even a young child can learn to help them stay safe. Faith in the Lord and yourself will save you. Mom and Dad, you both mean so much to me. I didn't hesitate to risk my life to be back with you because without you…I'm not me!"

The End

About the Author

Authors Juicy Fruitful Words
"Bully's are everywhere,
big, small, young and old.
With God, confidence and courage,
you are your own superhero".

SuzyQ is Teresa A. Radcliff, the author of "Amy's Great Escape" lives on a small farm in a small town in Kentucky. Teresa and her husband Stevie have five awesome kids, Ricky, Amanda, Davey, Calvin and Susann.

Their fluffy white dogs, Casper and Wendy spend the day chasing chickens and barking at the cows.

One day, while enjoying a huge event, called "Thunder over Louisville," her daughter, Amanda, was lost in a crowd of thousands of people from all over the nation, at age 8. The family searched and searched with no sign of her anywhere. After about thirty minutes or so, Amanda finds them. She runs up and hugs her momma tight. Standing beside her was a police officer which Amanda found the moment she lost her family. Because Amanda did the right thing by seeking an officer at the beginning, she probably avoided the possibility of a dangerous situation. After the incident, the author of this book thought it would be helpful if kids learn at an early age how to stay calm and act responsibly.

After High School, Teresa attended Jefferson Community College and the University of Kentucky.

She currently works as a US mail carrier with the United States Postal Service. Prior, she worked for a short period in the US States Corrections Department, including a State Youth Program. Her experience is more prevalent during her career in the mental health and developmental disability field where she obtained knowledge, skills, and hands-on crisis management for over sixteen years.

After opening and operating her own state agency, she acquired great knowledge from attending many psychological evaluations. She instructed safe crisis management statewide and taught CPR and first aid for the American Red Cross in addition to other related experiences.

I Got Notes

CPSIA information can be obtained
at www.ICGtesting.com
Printed in the USA
BVHW021127030419
544437BV00003B/6/P